Down by the Barn

Written and Illustrated by
Will Hillenbrand

SCHOLASTIC INC.

ISBN 978-0-545-80557-5

12 11 10 9 8 7 6 5 4 3 2   14 15 16 17 18 19/0

Printed in the U.S.A.   40

First Scholastic printing, September 2014

The illustrations are mixed media.

Book design by Will Hillenbrand and Katrina Damkoehler

Editor: Margery Cuyler

To Dee,
and thanks to Rich

Down by the barn,
early in the morning,
see the little wagons
all in a row!

See the tractor driver
pull his little lever . . .

Puff, Puff,
click, clank,
OFF WE GO!

Down by the cows,
early in the morning,
see the little calf
waiting to go!

See the tractor driver
pull his little lever . . .

Puff, Puff,
click, clank,
moo, moo,
OFF WE GO!

Down by the chickens,
early in the morning,
see the little chick
waiting to go!

See the tractor driver
pull his little lever ...

Puff, Puff, click, clank,
moo, moo, peep, peep,
OFF WE GO!

Down by the pigs,
early in the morning,
see the little piglet
waiting to go!

See the tractor driver
pull his little lever . . .

Puff, Puff,
click, clank,
moo, moo,
peep, peep,
wee, wee,
OFF WE GO!

Down by the geese,
early in the morning,
see the little gosling
ready to go!

See the tractor driver
pull his little lever ...

puff, puff,
click, clank,
moo, moo,
peep, peep,
wee, wee,
honk, honk,
OFF WE GO!

Down by the sheep,
early in the morning,
see the little lamb
waiting to go!

See the tractor driver
pull his little lever ...

Puff, Puff, click, clank,
moo, moo, peep, peep,
wee, wee, honk, honk,
baa, baa,
OFF WE GO!

Down by the goats,
early in the morning,
see the little kid
waiting to go!

See the tractor driver
pull his little lever . . .

Puff, Puff,
click, clank,
moo, moo,
peep, peep,
wee, wee,
honk, honk,
baa, baa,
nay, nay,
OFF WE GO!

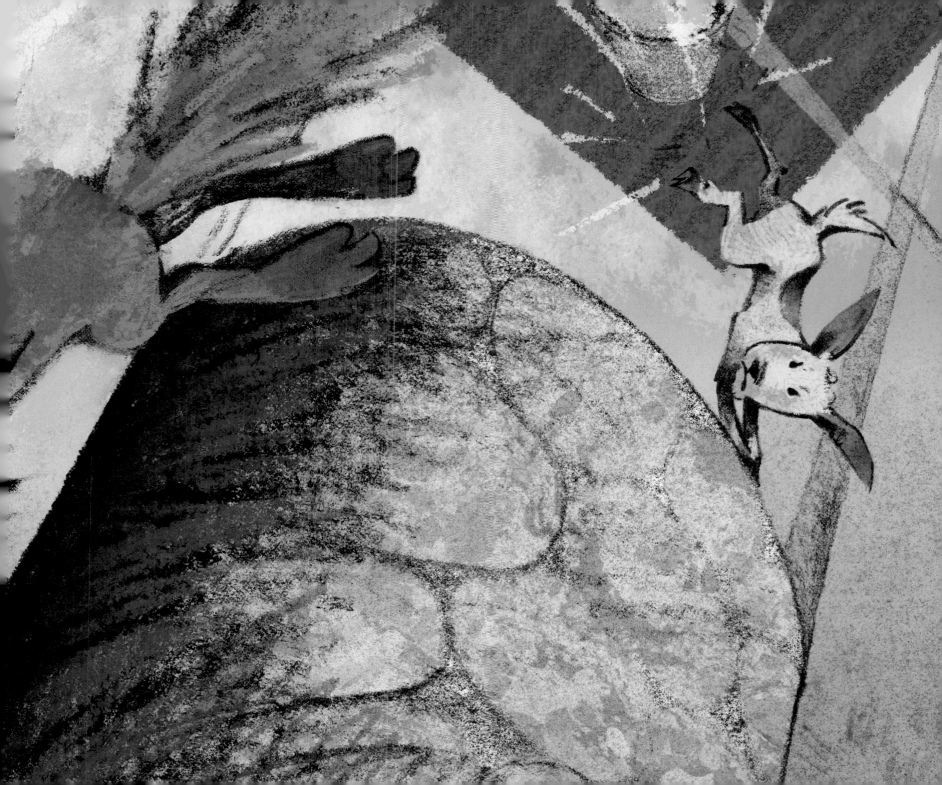

Down by the cats,
early in the morning,
see the little kitten
waiting to go!

See the tractor driver
pull his little lever . . .

Puff, Puff, click, clank,
moo, moo, peep, peep,
wee, wee, honk, honk,
baa, baa, nay, nay,
mew, mew, OFF WE GO!

Down by the children's barn,
early in the morning,
see the baby animals
exit in a row.

See the tractor driver
pull his little lever . . .

Puff, Puff,
click, clank,

HERE AT LAST!